The Castaway Mouse

The Castaway Mouse

ODDITY'S STORY

ANNE MERRICK
Pictures by Tessa Richardson-Jones

Bloomsbury

FOR LILY

First published in Great Britain in 1996
Text copyright © 1996 Anne Merrick
Illustrations © 1996 Tessa Richardson-Jones
The moral right of the author has been asserted
The moral right of the illustrator has been asserted

Bloomsbury Publishing PLC, 2 Soho Square, London W1V 6HB
A CIP catalogue record for this book is available from The British Library
ISBN 0 7475 2659 1 pb
ISBN 0 7475 2660 5 hb

10 9 8 7 6 5 4 3 2 1

Cover design by Alison Withey
Typeset by Hewer Text Composition Services, Edinburgh
Printed and bound by Caledonian International Book
Manufacturing, Glasgow

Key to mouse
Parlours
1 Uppity
2 Calamity
3 Homity and Dimity
4 Alacrity
5 Serenity
6 Curiosity
7 Serendipity
8 Dignity
9 Oddity
→ → → → Tracks

Wild Wood

4

Harry's room

5

Kitchen

7

Cellar

9

Underground Spring

The Village

Manor House

Attic

Jones's Bedroom

Parlour

Foundations

CHAPTER ONE

It was November.

In Mr and Mrs Jones's garden the trees stood shivering in the wind that tore the last leaves from their branches. Leaves danced across the lawn and drifted in heaps against the fence. They whirled into the yard and twirled into the corners. They flew over the roof and settled like rusty patches on the slates before slithering into the gutter.

Then the rain began.

Water streamed across the roof, spilled out of the choked-up gutter and splashed like a waterfall into the yard. The Jackdaw that always perched on the chimney pot squawked loudly and flapped away into the Wild Wood.

Mr Jones poked his head out of the kitchen door.

'Mrs Jones,' he said, 'it's raining cats! I don't think you should take the Dog for a walk today.'

'What!' barked the Dog. 'What! No walk!'

'Yo ho ho!' shrieked the Parrot from her cage. 'Storm to windward! Batten down the hatches!'

'Mr Jones,' said Mrs Jones, putting the kettle on the stove, 'come in out of the wet and toast some crumpets by the fire. The rain will have stopped by the end of the day.'

But the rain did not stop. Not that day. Nor the next. Nor the next after that.

Behind the walls and under the floors the Tribe of Mice who lived in every nook and cranny of the Jones's house listened to the rain falling.

'Oh dear! Oh deary!' sighed Homity from his cosy Parlour in the Attic. 'The world Outside seems to be MELTING!'

The Sparrows from Outside flew in under the eaves and stayed there shivering.

Homity's cousin, Uppity, went to look through one of the gaps under the slates. On clear days he could see right across the garden to the Water Meadows and the River. Sometimes he could even see as far as the Wild Wood. But all he could see today was a quilt of grey cloud with long, shining needles of rain tumbling out of it.

Through a chink between the tiles a heavy rain drop plopped on to Uppity's head and water from the blocked gutter slopped in under the eaves. The Attic floor was beginning to darken with patches of wet.

Pushing through the Sparrows, he went to inspect the water trough. The trough was a rusty old roasting tin that Mr Jones had placed under a broken slate to catch the drips when it rained. Usually it had just enough water in it to supply the needs of the up-and-coming young Mice who lived in the Attic but today it was so full that little waves were lapping at its brim.

'If it goes on raining for much longer,' Uppity said to the Sparrows, 'we shall have a Flood.'

The Sparrows fluffed out their feathers and looked glum.

Uppity decided he ought to go and warn Great-Great-Grandfather Serendipity. Serendipity was the oldest and largest and wisest of the Mice who lived in the Mousehold. Many, many moons ago he and his wife Charity had travelled through all the difficulties and dangers of the world until they arrived at the Jones's house.

As Uppity left the Attic and scurried down the secret track which wound down through the chimney wall to the kitchen, he wondered if Great-Great-Grandfather would know how to deal with a Flood. Serendipity remembered the past more clearly than he remembered yesterday and he loved to tell stories about it. But Uppity could not recall him ever talking about a Flood.

Close to the kitchen, the track came to a crossroads.

'Hi, Man!' drawled a voice from the shadows. 'Dig that old wolf-wind! He's huffing and puffing fit to blow the house down!'

Uppity stopped. His Uncle Serenity was lounging against the chimney and laughing to himself.

'It's not funny, Uncle,' said Uppity. 'If this weather doesn't change soon we're going to be *drowned* up in the Attic.'

'Well, don't get miserable, Man,' said Serenity. 'Crying will only add to the damp!'

He laughed again and began to nibble a nugget of Bonio he'd found in the Dog's bowl. It was hard to ruffle Uncle Serenity. He was the most carefree mouse in the Tribe.

'Potty old hippy mouse!' Uppity said as he hurried away. 'Or do I mean . . . old . . . hippy potty mouse?'

He was still trying to decide which order of words was best, and why the second one reminded him of something, when he arrived at the entrance to Serendipity's Parlour.

CHAPTER TWO

While all this was going on at the top of the house, deep down in the Foundations, Oddity sat alone in his Parlour. He lived in the Foundations because nobody else wanted to, which meant he had them to himself. Oddity did not much enjoy the company of other Mice.

When he was very young his brothers and sisters and cousins chased after him shouting, 'One blind Mouse! See how he runs!'

Or they danced round him chanting, 'You can't catch me – because you can't *see!*'

It was true that Oddity could not see as well as they could. He had been born with only one eye so that half of the world was always blank and dark to him. But inside his head Oddity saw other wonderful and mysterious worlds about which the other Mice knew nothing. And he spent a lot of his time daydreaming about them.

At this moment he was dreaming about Dimity. Dimity was Homity's sister and she lived with him in an old picnic basket in the Attic. As he thought about her, Oddity could see her quite clearly. Her honey-coloured fur was soft and silky. Her eyes shone with a gentle light and she had the daintiest pink ears he had ever seen.

Dimity never teased Oddity as the others did. She was too shy to speak up for him but whenever Uppity crept up on his blind side and shouted 'BOO!', or whenever Alacrity darted at him shouting, 'Now you see me, now you don't!', Dimity refused to join in. She knew what it was like to be teased.

'We're birdth of a feather,' she told him once. 'I can't thpeak properly and you can't thee properly. We're *both* odditieth!'

But underneath her shyness, Dimity was brave. In spite of being scared of the dark she came every day to visit him. And when she came she seemed to bring her own light with her. As she picked her way across the mounds of earth, between the heaps of bricks and stumps of wood that lay

everywhere in the Foundations, she flickered like a small, golden flame.

Today, however, Oddity hoped she would not come. For some time he had heard water gurgling and gushing beneath him but now, as he came out of his daydream about Dimity, he realised the sound had grown much louder. He listened for a while and then started to compose a rhyme.

'You are my moonshine,' he sang, 'my only
 moonshine!
You make me happy when times are black.
One day you'll know, dear, how much I love
 you,
But just for now, dear – please don't come back!'

When he had finished singing, Oddity stood up.
His Parlour was built in the roots of the old apple
tree that grew in the yard. The roots had broken
through the wall into the Foundations just above
the place where a little spring welled up out of the
earth. They were slimy with wet, and white with
mould, and in the spaces between them there were
caverns that were blacker than the inside of Mr
Jones's boots.

In the topmost of these caverns Oddity's home
was snug and dry. He had lined it with dry
leaves and wisps of straw and the stream beneath it usually trickled safely away into the
garden through a low archway in the wall. But
today the water was flowing so fast and so high
that Oddity could hear it sloshing in and out of
the lower caves. It made him feel as if his
Parlour was about to slip its moorings and sail
off with him.

He went out on to the branch that made a balcony in front of his Parlour and peered into the blackness. The waves licked up at him, glittering with their own dark light. By it he could see that the water was starting to spread across the Foundations. He must stay and watch for Dimity. Warn her that there was a deep lake all around the tree root.

Settling down with his back to his Parlour wall, he cheered himself up by composing another rhyme.

'With a heigh-ho,' he sang, 'the wind
    and the rain
I wish that they would go away.
There's going to be a Flood again
If the rain just rains on every day!'

Oddity could not remember there ever being a Flood before. But high up on the walls of the Foundations he had seen the wavy white lines which showed where, long ago, the stream had risen and left its mark.

To keep himself awake as time passed and the waves surged among the roots below him, he sang his rhyme over and over again.

CHAPTER THREE

'Grandad wants *everyone* to come to a Meeting in the Attic,' Uppity told all his uncles and aunts and cousins. 'There's going to be a Flood and we are in a most Dangerous Situation!'

While Uppity took this message round the Mousehold, Great-Great-Grandfather Serendipity left his Parlour behind the stove in the kitchen and began the long journey to the top of the house. The secret passageways used by the Mice wound everywhere through the walls but the chimney track went directly from the Foundations up to the roof. It was fairly straight but very steep and nowadays Serendipity could only climb it slowly.

'You're getting too old for this, Father,' panted Dignity, his eldest son, who went up with him. 'It's time you let me take over.'

But Serendipity loved Meetings. He enjoyed lecturing his Family as much as he enjoyed telling them stories. When at last he arrived in the Attic he took a deep breath and then strolled among the heaped-up boxes and ramshackle bits of furniture that Mr and Mrs Jones stored there until he reached the tin trunk under the skylight.

Rain drummed on the slates and dripped through a crack in the skylight on to the lid of the trunk.

'Bah!' exclaimed Serendipity.

And instead of clambering up on to the trunk as he usually did, he took shelter under Mrs Jones's tattered blue umbrella which was propped against it. Squinting through the dim blue light he looked at the crowd of Mice gathering around him.

'My dear Children,' he began when they had settled down. 'In all my long life I have never myself experienced a Flood. But from the stories my Elders told me I know that once upon a time there was a Terrible Flood that drowned the whole world . . .'

'Hm,' murmured Dignity doubtfully. 'Indeed?'

Serendipity scowled. Sometimes he had no patience with his eldest son. Dignity was so unadventurous himself that he never quite believed in anybody else's adventures.

'The Tribe of Mousity,' he went on sternly, 'is only here today because a Human of those times built an Ark . . .'

'What's a Nark?' asked Uppity who was standing at the front.

'An Ark,' said Serendipity, 'is a boat. Or rather it's a sort of . . . floating house.'

'Our house is soon going to be a Nark then,' remarked Uppity, watching a little rivulet that was flowing down the umbrella and making a puddle on the floor. 'It's nearly afloat already!'

'But *this* one,' said Great-Great-Grandfather, 'was *meant* to float! And it was so huge that it could hold two of every kind of creature that lived on the earth at that time. Including even the monstrous Heffalumps. And the Hippopoto-mice . . .'

'Were there *ordinary* Mice like us as well?' asked Uppity.

'Of course,' said Serendipity. 'And as everybody knows, two Mice soon make four and four Mice make eight and eight Mice make . . .'

Uppity was trying to work out the arithmetic of this when Uncle Serenity, who hated Meetings, yawned loudly.

'Man!' he said. 'Don't get unbelievable! Mice might be great at multiplication but whoever heard of a Mouse building a boat?'

Serendipity sighed. If his eldest son was a bore, he thought, his youngest was a fool. Waving one paw at the lumber all around them he spoke loudly and slowly as though the whole of his family was deaf.

'WOOD,' he said, 'FLOATS. And here in this Attic there are drawers made of wood, boxes made of wood, crates made of wood . . . We don't have to BUILD an Ark. We are surrounded by them!'

The other Mice stared up at him with rounded eyes.

'There is even,' Serendipity continued more quietly, 'a wooden house. The Doll's House. Where I believe my dear grandson Uppity has his Parlour.'

Uppity's tail twitched. He did not like the idea of turning his own Parlour into a Nark.

Dimity, who was standing beside him, only half listened to Serendipity. She was watching the waves wobbling at the rim of the water trough. As another rain drop plinked into it and one of the waves toppled over the edge she squeaked with fright and covered her eyes with her paws.

'What about Oddity?' she cried. 'Where ith he? Did you go down to the Foundationth, Uppity, and tell him about . . .?'

'Do shut up Dim-Witty,' said Uppity. 'You sound just like Curiosity throwing questions at me like that! Anyway, I don't want to talk. I want to think . . .'

'If the thream in the Foundationth overflowth,' moaned Dimity, 'it'th poor Oddity who'll *think*!'

Another wave washed over the side of the trough.

'My dear children,' said Great-Great-Grandfather Serendipity. 'We must start to search for a suitable Ark.'

CHAPTER FOUR

Oddity woke with a start as water splashed up at him, soaking his fur. Creeping to the edge of his balcony he twisted his head this way and that to scan the Foundations with his one eye.

The light seeping in through air vents in the cellar floor was so feeble that usually it was lost in

the blackness of this underground place. But now Oddity could see faint sparks of it flaring on the water which had risen like a tide since he fell asleep. And along the farthest margin of the Flood where the waves were breaking in a line of foam Oddity thought he saw something move.

'Dimity!' he cried. 'Is that you?'

The something flitted to and fro, flickering in the darkness like a pale flame, and after a moment he heard her answering cry.

'There's water, water everywhere,' Oddity sang out. 'Don't try to cross – you'll sink. I'll swim over and meet you there. Quick as a flash – or a wink!'

The rhyme surprised him, coming into his head in the midst of such danger. He began to climb down through the tree root. The slapping of the water against its lower branches made it difficult to hear but he thought he heard Dimity calling to him to be careful. He knew every ledge and foot-hold on the way down but it was all much wetter than usual and very slippery.

Halfway down he met a family of Slugs who nested in the rotting wood at the bottom of the root.

'Sssssss,' they hissed as they slithered past him, 'Go back ssssstupid! You'll be ssssswissssled away by the wavesssss!'

Oddity took no notice. With his whiskers flutter-ing in the breeze that blew up off the water, he scrambled down the next drop. The Flood had shifted twigs and leaves and other litter from all over the Foundations and dumped them among the roots. There they had jammed together and formed a dam which changed the shape of the root and made the water rise still further.

Oddity stopped and considered how best to go

on. His one eye fixed on a pool of calm water which lay behind the place where the waves boiled under the archway. Nosing forward he reached for the next branch.

As he did so a piece of driftwood knocked hard against the tree root. Oddity wobbled and one of the twigs sticking out from the dam poked him under the ear. Before he knew what was happening, his paws skidded from under him and he was plunging head over heels into the water.

Gasping and struggling, he tried to swim.

'Dimity,' he cried. 'Dimity!'

Then the strong current seized him. Dragging him this way and that it buffeted the breath from his body until at last he grew too weak to fight. His paws stopped paddling, his eyes closed and the Flood swallowed him down.

CHAPTER FIVE

In the darkness, Dimity could not see what was happening but she heard Oddity's cries. She backed away as the waves came frothing towards her, threatening to encircle her. Already the ground beneath her was a bog. Mud oozed between her claws and sucked at her paws.

'Oddity!' she squealed.

But except for the rustling of the Flood among the bricks and stones, there was no answer. With her heart full of fear and sorrow Dimity waited. If,

as Oddity said, she brought light into the Foundations, perhaps he would see her and swim towards her. If he was *able* to swim . . .

But there was no further sound from Oddity. Dimity called again and again but all she heard was the surge of the water. The blackness of the Foundations seemed to press against her eyes like something solid. But when she closed her eyes it was worse. She thought she heard whisperings and stealthy movements as though Something were prowling around her in the darkness, waiting to pounce.

Opening her eyes she looked once more at the water. To her surprise she saw that the rippling edge of the waves had shrunk back a little. The Flood was retreating.

Slowly she turned round and made her way back to the Mousehole in the wall. She knew now that Oddity would not return. Her head felt numb, her heart felt cold and she hardly knew where she was going. But the twists and turns of the track brought her at last to Serendipity's Parlour behind the stove in the kitchen. In the corner she could see Serendipity lying on a scrap of red velvet that once, long ago, his wife Charity had nibbled out of the Jones's curtains.

'Grandad,' she whispered, 'I think Oddity . . . Oddity hath . . . I mean I think Oddity mutht have . . .'

The word she needed would not come out and, instead of helping her, Serendipity gave a loud snore. Because he was very old, Dimity did not like to wake him so she went on. Echoing down to her through the funnel of the chimney she could hear the cawing of the Jackdaw who always perched on the pot.

'Drowned!' he croaked. 'Dead. Drowned. Dead!'

When Dimity reached the Attic, Homity was not at home. She sniffed around their Parlour in the Picnic Basket. But the basketwork had got wet in the Flood and it smelled so strongly of willow sap that her brother's scent was wiped out.

Sometimes, when Dimity first woke up, the faint

wood-and-watery smell of the willow made her think she was lying under a tree Outside. She could even hear the whispering of the leaves and the singing of a river nearby. Usually she loved this feeling but today all thought of water made her tremble.

'What's up, Dim-Witty?' asked Uppity's voice from somewhere above her head. 'Where've you been all this time?'

Looking up, she saw him peering over the edge of an open drawer in the chest beside the basket.

'If you're looking for Homity,' he went on,

'we're all up here. Playing at Narks. Waiting for the Flood to float us off. But Homity's fretting because he thought you must be *drowned* already!'

He laughed and the dread-ful word spun in Dimity's head. There seemed to be a mist in the Attic because although the sky beyond the skylight was brightening with morning, Uppity looked very dim and faraway.

'No,' she said. 'I'm all right. And the Flood ith going down. But oh, Uppity, I think that Oddity hath gone with it.'

There was a long pause while Uppity stared down at her, waiting for her to explain.

'I think,' she mourned, 'that Oddity hath . . . drowned . . .'

CHAPTER SIX

After the water swallowed Oddity it sucked him under the archway in the wall and he knew nothing more until he found himself lying on his back with his nose in the air.

He was still in the water but he could breathe again. The water rocked him gently as it carried him along. High above him was the night sky. The rain had stopped, the clouds had gone and a million stars were winking down at him. Sleepily Oddity winked back.

Once upon a time Great-Great-Grandfather Serendipity had been lost in a sewer. He thought he was going to die down there in the dark when suddenly he saw two stars shining where no stars could possibly be. The stars did not keep still as they should but came shooting towards him. Then, as they drew near, they turned into the warm, bright eyes of Great-Great-Grandmother Charity . . .

'If only two of *you* turned out to be Dimity's eyes!' Oddity said to the stars in the sky. But the stars just went on winking and blinking and none of them moved.

'This is no good,' he said to himself. 'I must escape from this Flood!'

And rolling over he started to swim.

Instead of paddling through water, however, his paws scrabbled on something flat and hard. Realising he could stand up in an unsteady sort of way, he stopped trying to swim and sniffed carefully all around him. He discovered then that he was travelling on a plank of wood. The plank was about the size and shape of Mrs Jones's chopping board but its edges were rough and splintery. And in the middle, sticking up like a mast, there was a large nail.

As the plank started to pitch and toss over rough water, Oddity marvelled how he had come to be on board it at all. Perhaps the waves had flung him there? He peered into the starlit dark. The Flood stretched as far as he could see – and farther. What if his raft had carried him right out to Sea?

'Yo ho ho!' he said, remembering the words the Parrot used when she was practising to be a Pirate.

The rocking of the plank was making him feel drowsy so he lay down. Words floated lazily into his head and he began to sing.

> 'Yo ho ho and away I go
> To the lonely Sea and the sky.
> It's safer far to stay where I . . . are
> Till rescue comes by and by!'

The song lulled him to sleep. He dreamed that he and Dimity were travelling together to a magical land where all they had to do was link paws and they could fly like the Sparrows who flew in and out of the eaves. Swooping over hills and fields, over towns and gardens, they came at last to the edge of a great, green, glassy Flood. The Flood spread on and on until it met the sky. Dropping down on to the shore they stood and watched while the sun, like a fiery ball, rose slowly out of the waves . . .

Oddity's plank rammed into something, spun round three times and raced on faster than ever.

Sitting up he saw that the dawn had broken. His raft settled down again and Oddity looked about him. He was sailing between two grassy banks. On each side of him willow trees leaned out over their own reflections and trailed their snaky branches in the waves. Two brown ducks went wagtailing along under one bank and from the other a frog plopped softly into the water.

'Is this The Sea?' called Oddity as the frog swam past him.

'Never. Never. Never!' croaked the frog. 'It's the River. River. River.'

Oddity cleaned his face and preened his whiskers. Against a hazy blue sky the sun shone like the brass gong in the Jones's hall and it was already warm. He began to feel quite cheerful.

'The Sea would have been too big an adventure for a Mouse like me,' he said to himself. 'But sailing down the River on a pea-green raft is just right! It's the sort of adventure that should go down in history. Even Great-Great-Grandfather has never gone sailing!'

'Good morning,' he sang to a flock of Sparrows flying overhead. 'Good morning! Isn't it a lovely day?'

'Good morning,' chirped the Sparrows. 'Good morning to you!'

Oddity felt happy but he also felt hungry and there was nothing on his raft to eat. He could not find even a grain of wheat or a crumb of bread wedged in one of its cracks. He was just wondering whether to try gnawing at the plank itself, when the River gave it a mighty shove.

Oddity lost his balance and sprawled on the deck. The raft bumped and jolted as though it were being hauled over rocks and then the whole

world seemed to turn topsy turvy. Through a
fountain of spray he saw the land disappear
altogether. Digging his claws into the wood while
the world did another great somersault, he clung
on. River and sky changed places. Out of his one
eye Oddity saw something huge and black loom
above him. Then the raft struck the something,
bounced twice, and stuck fast.

Shaken loose by the collision Oddity's claws
squealed across the wood. He tried to whip his
tail round the mast to hold him but he was falling

too fast. His paws beating helplessly at the air he roly-polied down the slope of the plank and – for the second time that day – he tumbled headfirst into the water.

CHAPTER SEVEN

'A Mouse all alone fell into the Flood
From his beautiful pea-green raft.
And all the birds in the tree above
Just laughed and laughed and laughed!'

Oddity beat his paws to mark the rhythm of his rhyme.

He was sitting on a small pebbly beach. Behind him was the alder tree whose black roots had ship-wrecked his raft. And perched all along its branches were the Sparrows who had overtaken him on his voyage. They were still twittering merrily, as they had been doing ever since he crawled up through the roots and found his way ashore.

'Isn't it a lovely day?' they sang. And they twittered again.

Oddity did not answer. To him the day did not seem quite as lovely as before. He was weary from his struggle to escape the River, and weak from hunger.

'Food,' he muttered. 'I must find food.'

He set off across the Pebbly Beach. Where the shore ended there was a rocky cliff. It was about the height of the Jones's kitchen table and at the top of it Oddity could see a thicket of young trees. Bramble and brier rose twined together among hawthorn and hazel and mountain ash. There were plenty of footholds in the rock and in spite of his tiredness it did not take him long to climb up.

From the stories and legends of his Tribe, Oddity knew that there were many Monsters living in such places. Monsters who were the sworn enemies of Mice. But the thicket smelled only of leaf mould and the coming of Winter and his keen nose could not detect any danger. Soon he was nibbling a tasty rosehip and exploring a little further he found several hawthorn berries and half a hazelnut.

When he was full he returned to the Alder Tree. The black roots twisting out over the water reminded him of home. Between the roots there were cushions of spongy green moss and settling himself there Oddity listened to the River. A yellow leaf drifted past him like a sigh. Across the sparkling water he could see a field where black and white cows munched dreamily in the sun. Nowhere in the Jones's house had he ever seen such brightness or such colours . . .

Because it was November, however, the sun went down early. As it dipped behind the alder tree shadows sprang up everywhere and the brightness faded. Mist curling up from the River mingled with the shadows and Oddity shivered. He had never before been out in the Wilderness. He had never before been Outside at night!

'Beware of the Nose of the Fox, the Ears of the Stoat and the Eye of the Owl.'

Great-Great-Grandfather Serendipity's words came suddenly into his head and made his heart beat fast. Low in the sky the Evening Star flickered

like a silver flame and he thought again of Dimity. He thought too of his snug little Parlour in the Foundations and for the first time he felt homesick.

'The water came in and the water went out
And swept it all away.
It won't be fit to live in again
For many and many a day.'

Although the song was a sad one, singing it cheered Oddity up and he went on humming it while he searched for a safe place where he could spend the night. He had already noticed that half-way up the cliff there was a ledge which zigged and zagged across the rock face until it disappeared under a curtain of ivy.

In the green twilight he nosed along the ledge. Spiders he disturbed snarled at him before scuttling crossly away. Snails, clinging to the undersides of the ivy leaves, drew in their horns and played dead. But at last he found what he was searching for.

Where the ledge widened in the middle of the ivy patch, there was a deep slit in the cliff face. Testing the slit with his whiskers he felt it was just wide enough for him to wriggle into. And when the whole of him was inside he discovered to his delight that the slit opened up and became a cave.

A last gleam of daylight slanting in through the ivy shone like a torch beam into the cave. The floor was covered with soft, dry sand. The walls were speckled with golden lichen. And the roof was domed like the inside of Mrs Jones's pudding basin.

Oddity scratched some grass seeds out of his coat and nibbled them. Then, scooping a little hollow in the sand, he lay down. Neither the Nose of the Fox, the Ears of the Stoat nor the Eye of the Owl would find him here.

'Tomorrow,' he said to himself, 'I'll find my way home to the Jones's house. If Great-Great-Grand-father Serendipity could do it – so can I!'

Beyond the scurryings of small creatures in the ivy and the sighing of the breeze in the thicket he could hear the River singing an endless lullaby.

'All I have to do,' he murmured sleepily, 'is to follow the River. In no time at all I'll be back with Dimity!'

CHAPTER EIGHT

While the other Mice slept tight in their Parlours after the alarms of the Flood, Dimity moped. She could not sleep, because every time she dozed off she heard Oddity crying to her or saw the black waters swirling him away.

'He might be all right, you know,' said Curiosity, who had come up to the Attic to see what was going on now that the rain had stopped. 'On my very first Quest I fell into a drain and a torrent of water carried me off. But I didn't *drown*. I found out how to swim. I wonder if something like that has happened to Oddity? Where does the stream in the Foundations *go?* D'you think it might have taken him to Outside?'

But Dimity did not know. Leaving her cousin she went down once more to the Foundations. The Flood had dwindled to a puddle but the ground was very boggy and it took her a long time to reach the tree root. Afraid of what she might find, Dimity took little frightened peeps under the root and into the black water. But there was no sign of Oddity. And when she called his name it echoed

42

emptily back at her from under the arch. Perhaps Curiosity was right and he had been swept away to Outside.

Much later, when she returned to the Attic, she found everyone in a state of excitement.

'Mr Jones has been up here,' explained Uppity. He was leaning against the verandah of the Doll's

House chatting to some of the other up-and-coming young Mice.

'Oh dear!' exclaimed Homity, wringing his paws. 'What if he *noticed* us!'

'Old Jonesy's as blind as the bats up in the rafters,' scoffed Uppity. 'We could play Tag over his toes – as we do with the Dog – and he wouldn't see us!'

'What did he come here *for*?' asked Curiosity. 'Was he running away from Mrs Jones? Was she cross with him? Why did . . .?'

'Do shut up, Ossy,' said Uppity. 'You ask so many questions you never leave space for the answers!'

'I only wanted to know, you know,' she said, tossing her head.

'Hickory, dickory!' said Alacrity. 'Get on with the story! Mr Jones was fussing about the Flood. He emptied the water trough and mended the crack in the skylight . . .'

'*And* he stuffed paper into the gaps under the eaves . . .'

The Mice glanced at the Sparrows who were gossiping together around the water trough.

'What about them?' asked Curiosity. 'How can they fly out again if the holes are blocked?'

'Easy peasy,' chirped the Sparrows. They started to hop about under the eaves, pecking at the bungs of paper.

Dimity wandered away from her cousins and went to look out through the first gap the Sparrows had cleared. She stared across the Water Meadows where the River had spread until it lay like a lagoon between the Jones's garden and the Wild Wood.

'Oh, poor Oddity,' she mourned, 'how could you pothibly ethcape from all that water!'

One of the Sparrows paused in his busy shredding of the paper.

'Did you say Oddity?' he cheeped. 'Is that what you call the One-Eyed One?'

'Yeth,' said Dimity.

'Then poor Oddity, my claw!' said the Sparrow. 'He's far away – and fancy free . . .'

'Underneath the alder tree,' said one of the others and they all chirruped with laughter, remembering how Oddity had rhymed about *them*.

Dimity's heart fluttered. If the Sparrows had seen a one-eyed Mouse who spoke in rhyme then it *had* to be Oddity. She asked them to tell her exactly where they had seen him. It took them ages because they all talked at once and by the time they finished Curiosity had come over to see what they were talking about.

'How far away is that?' she asked. 'How long does it take to get there?'

'A thousand wing beats, said one Sparrow.

'From first light to sunrise,' said another.

'It would take much longer for me,' said Dimity. 'Becauthe I can't fly.'

'Dimity!' exclaimed Curiosity. 'Are you really going on a *Quest*? Can I come with you? I'm good at Quests and I'd like to know . . .'

But Dimity shook her head. She was filled with a strange new daring.

'I want to go by mythelf,' she said. 'Oddity will need me. Jutht ath Great-Great-Grandfather needed Great-Great-Grandmother Charity . . .'

While Curiosity scurried away to investigate the trail of a black beetle, and the Sparrows went on dismantling Mr Jones's flood defences, Dimity gazed at the vastness of Outside.

'When the Flood'th gone down and the River ith back,' she said, 'I'll go and find him . . .'

CHAPTER NINE

The sun rose and set six times while Oddity trekked along the River Bank. It was a long and difficult journey. In places the River was too wide for him to see land on the other side. In other places the thickets were so dense that he emerged from them torn and bleeding. And for one whole day he teetered along on the edge of a precipice that dropped sheer to the foaming water below.

In all that time he met neither friend nor enemy. Occasionally he saw the Sparrows flying high

overhead and once, as he was crossing a grassy plain where mounds of earth rose like crumbly hills all round him, an animal rose straight out of the ground under his nose.

'Hallo!' said Oddity, who was so pleased to see someone that he forgot to be wary. 'Who are you?'

The animal's coat was as black as the coal in the Jones's Outhouse. Its cherry-red nose snuffed the air and its eyes, buried deep in its fur, squinted at him disagreeably.

'Clear off!' it growled. 'You're trespassing among my diggings!'

'But who . . .?' persisted Oddity. He felt sorry for a creature whose two eyes seemed less good than his one.

'Mole,' grunted the animal. 'Mole . . . Mole . . . Mole . . . Mo . . .'

By the time it reached the last word the Mole had already disappeared. It dug itself into the earth as fast as a frog dives into water. But although the Mole was so unfriendly Oddity felt lonelier than ever after it had gone. To banish the loneliness, he started to compose a new rhyme as he went on his way.

'Mole! Mole!' he chanted. 'Down with Mole!
Down with the crabby, cantankerous Mole!
I'd rather meet a Mouse – or a Shrew – or a Vole
Than a grumpy old Mole whose home is a hole!'

He was still singing this marching song
when he turned a corner and found
himself on a stony beach. His march
and his song came to a sudden stop.
Ahead of him was an Alder Tree

with its roots in the water. Beyond the tree was a low cliff draped in ivy. And the stones beneath his paws were the yellow stones of the Pebbly Beach where he had first landed.

The River had led him in a circle.

For the rest of that day, Oddity sat and rested on the moss under the Alder Tree.

'I am a castaway,' he said to himself. 'I shall never get home.'

He knew now that he had been shipwrecked on an Island. And from his journey along the river-bank he also knew he could never escape. The water around the Island was too fast-flowing and the shores of the mainland too far away for him to swim.

He tried to remember if Great-Great-Grandfather Serendipity had ever told a story about being marooned on an island but none came into his head.

'Anyway,' he said to himself. 'I am not like Serendipity. I am not an adventurous Mouse . . .'

The reflection of the rising moon twinkled up at him from the River.

'But what has happened,' he said, 'has happened. If I am trapped on this Island I shall start tomorrow and explore the rest of it . . .'

The River chuckled and a solitary pink cloud drifted slowly across the sky. Watching it, Oddity felt another rhyme shaping itself in his head.

'I wandered lonely as the cloud
That floats above my Island home,' he murmured.
I don't care tuppence for the crowd
I *like* to be here on my own!'

It was just as well that Oddity did not mind being alone. In the following days while he wandered all over the Island he never once met another Mouse. Yet there were enough berries, nuts and seeds to feed a whole Tribe of them.

Under the Great Oak Tree in the middle of the Island there were hundreds of fallen acorns. And on the far side of his thicket there was a patch of wild barley, its whiskery seed heads still heavy with grain. He ate so much that he grew quite plump. His scratches healed and his coat became sleek and shiny. What's more, because he lived in the daylight instead of the dark, the sight of his eye improved.

Oddity began to feel he had always known this Island. It was like a place he had often visited in dreams but then, on waking, forgotten. Each night when he returned to his cave in the cliff, he thought it was the safest, snuggest, prettiest Parlour in the world. He caught no whiff of Fox or Stoat. And the only owls he heard stayed far away in the Wild Wood. Best of all, the music of the River made rhymes hop and skip in his head like never before.

As the days grew shorter and colder and he spent more time curled up in his Parlour, the memory of the Jones's house and of his tree root home in the Foundations faded to a shadow.

He did not, however, forget Dimity.

Night and day she haunted his dreams. Sometimes at dusk, when he went to forage in the thicket, he thought he saw a flicker of gold in the undergrowth, as though she were waiting for him there. Once or twice in the stillness of the night he was sure he heard her calling to him. He was happier than he had ever been in his life. But his constant longing for Dimity gave a note of sadness to his happiest songs.

CHAPTER TEN

Early one morning Oddity went down to the Pebbly Beach. As he brushed through the cobwebs strung between the ivy stems their frosted threads snapped with a tinkling sound. The cold air fizzed in his nose, filling him with energy.

He started to frolick along the sand. Ice crackled under his paws and suddenly he slipped and fell into a hole. When he climbed out of it he saw that there were lots more holes on the water's edge and that they had all been made by the paws of some large animal.

'By the twitching of my tail,' he muttered in alarm. 'Something wicked's on my trail!'

He sniffed at the paw prints but the smell that came off them was not frightening. It was somehow familiar. He puzzled over this mystery for the rest of that day. By sunset he decided the only way to solve it was to keep a lookout for the animal who had made the marks. And so, before the sun rose again, he was waiting on the ledge outside his Parlour.

Hidden behind the ivy with his eye to a peephole between the stems he watched the Pebbly Beach. He did not have to wait long. The sun was just touching the waves with gold when, from the field on the other side of the River, he heard a galumphing sound.

Oddity quivered as the noise drew nearer and grew louder. Then, on the far bank, a dog came bounding into sight. The dog was leaping up and down around two Human legs. Oddity could not see the rest of the Human but as the legs stopped on the top of the bank something stirred in his memory.

Before he had time to consider what it was, the dog barked and then a stick whirred through the air towards the Island. It fell short of the beach and splashed into the River. The dog romped down the bank and plunged into the water.

The River kept snatching the stick away but at last the dog grabbed it and bounded up on to the Pebbly Beach. As soon as Oddity saw it so close and so clear he knew at once why the smell of its paws had been familiar.

'It's the Dog-Who-Lives-In-A-Basket!' he said.

And with the name other memories came flooding back. He saw the Jones's house and smelled the warm cooking smells of the kitchen. He saw the Parrot hanging upside down in her cage and heard Great-Great-Grandfather's gruff warnings. And as he crouched quivering on the ledge outside his cave, the faraway voices of all his Tribe reached out to Oddity . . .

The Dog shook himself and the spray flying from his coat made rainbows dance in the sun. Then Mrs Jones called across the water and picking up his stick he swam back to her.

When they had both disappeared, Oddity scurried down to the beach. For a long time he stood and listened to the River and watched the waves crinkling in and out on the shore. Then he began a new song.

'I've been away for a month and a day,
In this land where the Oak Tree grows.
And here in this Wood
I hoped that I should
Begin a new Tribe – and stay!'

But without Dimity he would be alone for ever. Without Dimity there would be no new Tribe. And without Dimity, no matter how much he loved the Island, he knew now that he could not stay.

CHAPTER ELEVEN

The Dog-Who-Lived-In-A-Basket did not believe in Mice. Even when a Mouse popped up under his nose or ran over his toes, he did not see or feel it. Oddity knew this. And it was what gave him his Great Idea for getting back home.

In the quietness of his Parlour he thought about the Idea until he had worked it out in detail. It made him restless and excited and frightened and happy. It also made him sad.

For the next two mornings he kept a lookout on his ledge. But each day it rained and the Dog did not come. Then, on the third morning, it was misty and moisty but fine.

As he waited, Oddity scratched first one ear and then the other.

'Come on, sweet Do-og-gie,' he hummed. 'Coming for to carry me home!'

His eye ached with watching and the hairy stems of the ivy tickled his nose and made him sneeze. At last, in the distance, he thought he heard a

The Castaway Mouse

heavy swish-thump, swish-thump. The sound of a Human walking across grass.

Poking his head out through the leaves he sniffed the air. He could hardly bear it in case the swish-thump was not Mrs Jones's swish-thump. But soon there was the sound of a dog barking and not long after that he caught the scent of Mrs Jones.

Oddity looked back once at his Parlour in the rock and then with a twirl of his tail he scampered down the cliff. After two days of rain, the River was flowing faster than ever and the land on the other side was invisible in the mist.

'Will I be *brave* enough for this?' Oddity wondered aloud.

His words seemed to disturb something on the far bank. He heard pattering sounds as if small stones were rolling down the slope and dropping into the River. Then the branches of the Alder Tree creaked and the Dog yapped again. In the silence which followed he thought he heard a voice speaking to him out of the mist.

'Oddity?' said the voice. 'Are you there?'

Oddity's heart, already unsteady, nearly stopped beating altogether.

'Oh dear,' the voice went on. 'I wonder if thith ith the right plathe . . .'

Not far away now Oddity could hear the Dog blundering through the reed beds, rattling the dry stalks.

'Dimity!' he cried.

For a moment the River itself seemed to stop singing and hold its breath. And then, quite plainly, he heard her answer.

'Oddity! Oh Oddity! You are there! Tho the Thparrowth were right . . .'

'Of course we were right!' chirped the Sparrows who had just arrived. Fluttering their feathers they settled in the Alder Tree, tutting that they were not as bird-brained as they looked.

'It'th taken me thuch a long time to find the Island,' cried Dimity. 'And now I'm here the water'th too deep and I can't reach you. I can't even *thee* you!'

Frisking about with excitement Oddity tried to tell her everything at once. He tried to tell her how he loved the Island but how he loved her even more. He tried to tell her how, with the help of the Dog-Who-Lived-In-A-Basket, he planned to escape.

Dimity listened. Across the River the Island seemed to float in the mist like an enchanted Island. She had never seen anything so beautiful. And although Uppity called her Dim-Witty, she was really very clever. Oddity was not making much sense but she understood everything that he was trying to say. Most of all she understood that he loved the Island and did not really want to leave it.

She could hear the Dog snuffling towards her through the grass. She was afraid of the dark and afraid of water but she was not at all afraid of *him*. Keeping very still she waited on the bank. She said nothing to Oddity but let him go on talking.

The Human footsteps came closer and closer. By the time they stopped Mrs Jones was almost treading on Dimity's tail and the Dog was barking and bouncing around them both. Squeezing herself up as small as she could, Dimity gathered all her

strength together. Mrs Jones stooped, picked up a stick and threw it into the River. And as the Dog raced down the bank after it, Dimity jumped.

Her claws tangled in the Dog's long tail and she was waved about in the air like a flag. Then icy water was foaming all round her and she could hear nothing except its roar, see nothing except its blackness. Just as she thought she could not hold on a moment longer, the Dog pranced out of the River.

He shook himself and Dimity's claws slid out of his tail. The rising sun pierced the mist and turned the spray to rainbows. Dimity soared through them and came flickering down while the Dog went barking away across the Pebbly Beach. She landed on the cushions of green moss under the Alder Tree and lay there listening to the Sparrows cheering on its branches. Then Oddity was beside her, whispering to her, nuzzling her, making sure she was all right.

The Sparrows cheered louder than ever and from the topmost twig of the Great Oak a blackbird sang a song of welcome to the dawn.

But all that Dimity heard as she sat up and carefully preened her whiskers was Oddity's own song of delight as he welcomed her home to his Island.

The Castaway Mouse

The Castaway Mouse

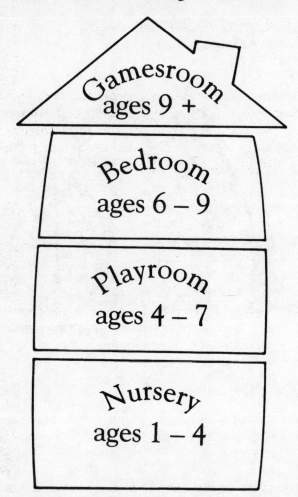

Gamesroom
ages 9 +

Bedroom
ages 6 – 9

Playroom
ages 4 – 7

Nursery
ages 1 – 4

Our Bloomsbury Book House has a special room for each age group – this one is from the Bedroom.

Watch out for more MOUSE TALES by Anne Merrick:

THE MOUSE WHO WANTED TO KNOW
07475 2641 9 hb/2615 X pb
£6.99 hb/3.99 pb

Meet Curiosity, the mouse who always wants to know everything! Join her in a series of tail-curling adventures as she sets out on a quest for knowledge in the terrifying outside world. Curiosity meets a most dangerous enemy, makes a life-long friend and brings Great Honour on the Tribe of Mousity.

A MESSAGE FROM A MOUSE
0 7475 2640 0 hb/2614 1 pb
£6.99 hb/3.99 pb

Up in the Smallest Bedroom lives Alacrity, the fastest mouse on four legs. When the Jones's house is invaded by a Boy, it is Alacrity who must find a way to deal with the Dangerous Situation that develops.

A MOUSE IN WINTER
0 7475 2662 1 hb/2661 3 pb
£6.99 hb/3.99 pb

Almost everyone in the Tribe of Mousity believes that Uppity is the boldest and bravest of the up-and-coming young Mice. As Mr and Mrs Jones prepare for Christmas, strange things begin to happen. Join Uppity as his courage is put the test in fighting an uncanny Christmas gift.

MORE BOOKS FROM THE BLOOMSBURY BEDROOM

Why not try: THE EXTRAORDINARY
LIGHTEN-ING CONDUCTOR.
0 7475 2076 hb/2204 9 pb
£6.99 hb/ 3.99 pb
Written by Nicola Matthews
Illustrated by Rachel Pearce

Imagine you've just woken up, and instead of being neatly tucked up in bed, you're floating above it! Is it a dream? Not for Greg, the boy in this story it isn't. Befriended by a mysteriously understanding dinner lady, he comes to terms with his gift and becomes a hero in front of the whole school.

Or try:
The TWO NAUGHTY ANGELS series.

DOWN TO EARTH.
ISBN 0 7475 2176 X hb/2121 2 pb
£6.99 hb/3.99 pb

THE GHOUL AT SCHOOL
ISBN 0 7475 2177 8 hb/2175 1 pb
£6.99 hb/3.99 pb
Written by Mary Hooper
Illustrated by Lesley Harker

What would it be like to have angels at your school? Has the new girl been behaving just a little bit too well? You had better look out, she might have escaped from heaven like the two angels in these books. With the Archangel after then, determined to force them back to a life of looking angelic with no fun whatsoever, the angels are constantly trying not to be discovered in the school they literally crashed into!